MW01061731

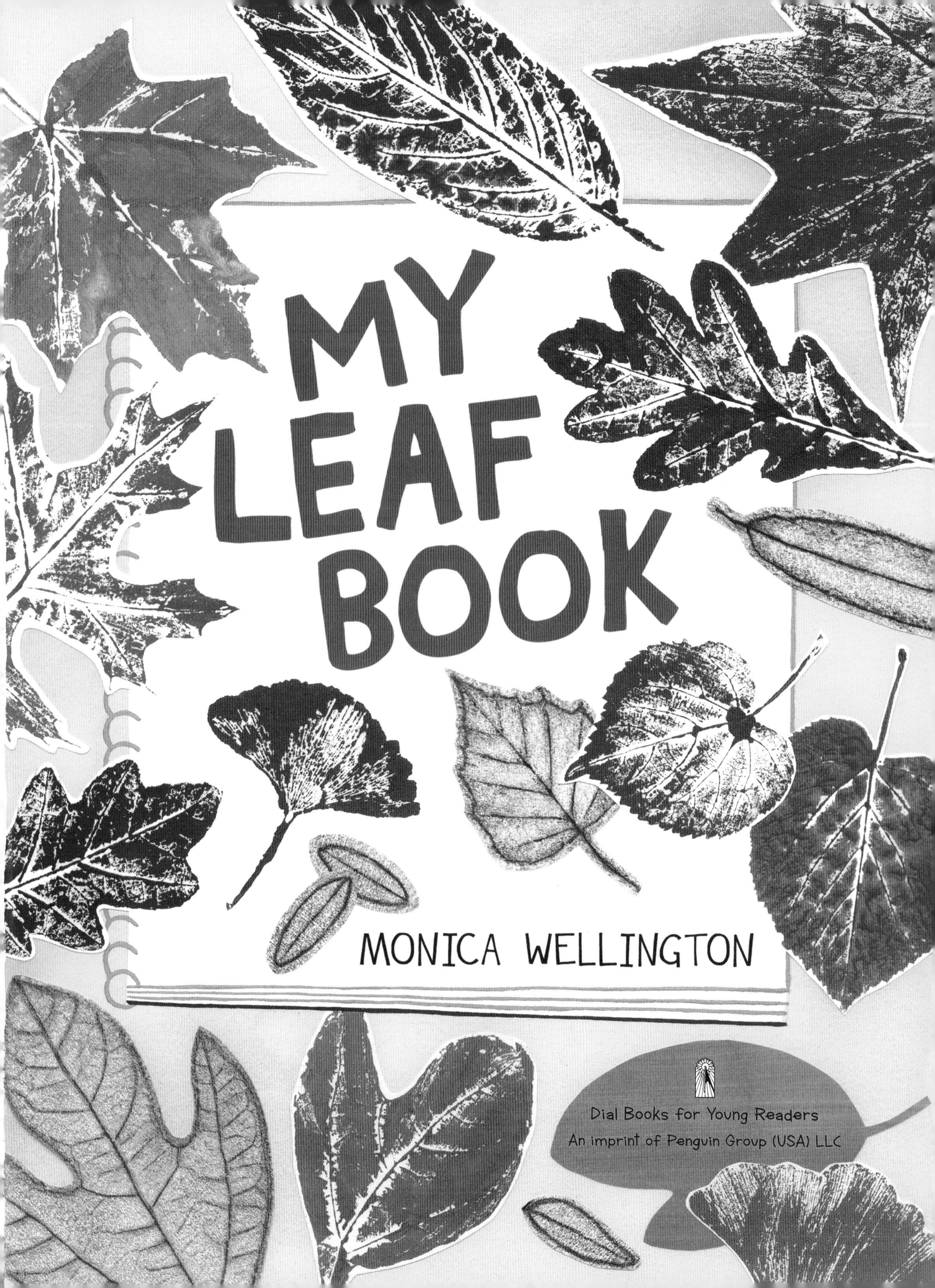

MY LEAF BOOK

MONICA WELLINGTON

Dial Books for Young Readers
An imprint of Penguin Group (USA) LLC

DIAL BOOKS FOR YOUNG READERS
Published by the Penguin Group
Penguin Group (USA) LLC
375 Hudson Street
New York, New York 10014

USA / Canada / UK / Ireland / Australia / New Zealand / India / South Africa / China
penguin.com
A Penguin Random House Company

Library of Congress Cataloging-in-Publication Data
Wellington, Monica, author, illustrator.
My leaf book / by Monica Wellington.
pages cm
Summary: "A young girl visits an arboretum in the autumn to collect fallen leaves. She identifies various trees by the shapes of their leaves and pastes her collection into her own leaf book."—Provided by publisher.
ISBN 978-0-8037-4141-6 (hardcover)
[1. Leaves—Fiction. 2. Trees—Fiction. 3. Autumn—Fiction.] I. Title.
PZ7.W4576My 2015 [E]—dc23 2014038487

Manufactured in China on acid-free paper
1 3 5 7 9 10 8 6 4 2
Designed by Jasmin Rubero
Text set in Clever Duke BTN Smooth

The pictures in this book are mixed-media collages, with various papers painted with gouache and acrylic. Autumn leaves were collected and used for prints, rubbings, and photocopies following the steps described at the end of this book. The collage elements were cut with scissors and pasted with glue. A computer was not used to create the artwork.

So many trees, so many leaves.
When the trees change colors, autumn is here,
and I go to the park to see
how many different leaves I can find.

Leaves are falling from the trees.

I want to collect as many as I can.

I catch my **first one!**

I am going to start a leaf book.

Here is my book.

Here is my Tree Guide.

And here is the leaf. It is shaped like a fan.

I use my Tree Guide to look for a match.

I find it: ginkgo leaf.

Leaf shape is a good place to start in identifying trees. Ginkgo leaves look like fans. The ginkgo is the oldest tree on Earth. It has existed for millions of years.

Some leaves are still on the trees. Some are on the ground.

I gather more leaves for my book. What is this one?

This leaf has five points.
It is shaped like a star.
It is from the **sweet gum** tree.

The **honey locust** tree
has millions of little leaves.

★ Most trees have simple leaves—a single leaf on each stalk, like sweet gum trees. Some have compound leaves—many leaflets on a stalk, like honey locust trees.

The wind blows this leaf right into my hand.

It is an oak leaf—a small reminder for my book of that big, beautiful tree.

Oak leaves are strong. They are good for my art projects. I make leaf rubbings in many colors.

I make **oak leaf** prints for my book, too.

Some leaves have lobes. This leaf above has seven, and the lobes are rounded. Other types of oaks have leaves with pointed lobes. Sweet gum leaves have pointed lobes, too.

Trees have different shapes and different barks, too.

So many trees, so many leaves.

So many colors, too.

Here are leaves of

red and violet and orange.

What kind are they? So many clues to help me.

Now I have birch, willow, and cherry leaves to put in my book. I am careful with them, because they are getting dry and brittle.

★ Leaves have veins. Their pattern can look like a feather, as in these leaves, and in oak leaves, too. Sometimes veins radiate from the base of the leaf, as in sweet gum leaves.

Shapes, shapes, so many different shapes.
These are like hearts.

This tree has leaves that are not all the same shape.

Some are like mittens.

I add linden
and sassafras leaves
to my book.
Linden
glue

The edges of leaves are either smooth or toothed. The edges of linden leaves have teeth. The edges of sassafras leaves are smooth.

The days are getting shorter, and the air is getting colder. Autumn trees are glowing bright. This one is the most colorful of all.

It is a maple tree.

The **maple** leaves are splendid—every shade of red and orange I can imagine!

My leaf book is full.
I have found so many beautiful leaves.
Which is my favorite?

A tree can have both little leaves and big leaves. The shape of the leaves, the presence of lobes and teeth, and the pattern of the veins are better ways to help identify trees.

I love
them all!

I love
them all!

✱ Leaf Projects ✱

You can make a leaf book of your own by pasting leaves you have collected onto pages, identifying them, and labeling them. Here are other projects to do with leaves.

Leaf Rubbings

✱ Place your leaf on a piece of paper, with the underside of the leaf facing down. (The veins of the leaf are more prominent on the underside and will give a sharper rubbing.)

✱ Tape the stem of the leaf to the paper and carefully turn the paper over. With colored pencils or crayons, rub your pencil lightly on the paper, on top of the leaves.

✱ Watch the shape, outline, and vein structure of the leaf come through!

Leaf Prints

✱ Spread out newspaper and get your paints ready. A thick type of paint such as poster or acrylic paint is best.

✱ Put a leaf on the newspaper with the underside up (where the veins are more prominent). Paint the leaf and move it to clean newspaper.

✱ Place a piece of plain paper on top of the leaf.

✱ Hold the paper firmly and rub all over with your fingertips. Feel the leaf through the paper.

✱ Lift the paper to reveal your leaf print.

✱ If your leaf has enough paint, you can repeat to make another lighter impression. Or you can paint your leaf again for more prints.

You can also make color photocopies of your most beautiful leaves before they fade.

Cut out the leaves from your photocopies, rubbings, and prints to use for your own projects and leaf book!